Cataloging-in-Publication Data (by Cassidy Cataloging)

Otoshi, Kathryn
Zero / by Kathryn Otoshi -- San Rafael, CA: KO Kids Books, c2010.
   p. ; cm.
   ISBN: 978-09723946-3-5
   Summary: One character's search to find value in herself and in others.

   1. Values--Juvenile fiction. 2. Counting--Juvenile fiction.
   3. Courage--Juvenile fiction. 4. Social Skills--Juvenile fiction.
   5. [Values--Fiction. 6. Counting--Fiction. 7. Courage--Fiction.] I. Title.

PZ7.O8775 Z47 2010
[Fic]--dc22   1009

KO KIDS BOOKS
16 Baytree Rd.
San Rafael, CA 94903
www.kokidsbooks.com

Distributed by Publishers Group West
www.pgw.com 1-800-788-3123

10 9 8 7 6 5 4 3 2

Printed in China

ZerO

by Kathryn Otoshi

But how could a number worth nothing become something?

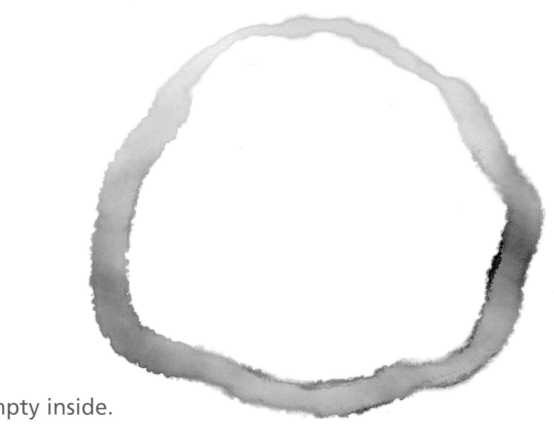

Zero felt empty inside.

Every day she watched the numbers line up.

She wanted to **count** too.

When she looked at herself,
she just saw a hole...right in her center.

Zero was a big round number.

She watched **One** having fun with the others.

One was solid and strong with bold strokes and squared corners.

Zero was big and round with no corners at all.

"If I were like One, then I could count too!" she thought.

So she *pushed* and pulled,

she stretched and STRAIGHTENED,

she FORCED and FLATTENED and finally became…

She sighed. Becoming like **One** was too much of a stretch.

Eight and **Nine** rolled into the scene.
"If you doubled yourself up, you'd be like me!" said **Eight**.
So **Zero** twisted and turned to try to be **Eight**.

"Or you could be a Nine with a longer line," said **Nine**.
So **Zero** pinched and puckered to try to be **Nine**.

But **Zero** could only be **Zero**.

"We're on our way to join the others.
Come count with us!" they said.

Zero felt deflated.
Eight and Nine were numbers with **value**.
Of course they'd **count**. How could they know how she felt?

Zero had a new thought.

If she could *impress* the numbers, that'd give her **value**.

She'd leap, she'd soar, she'd sizzle, she'd shine.

She'd make a grand entrance and floor them all!

and **faster...**

Zero began to roll **faster...**

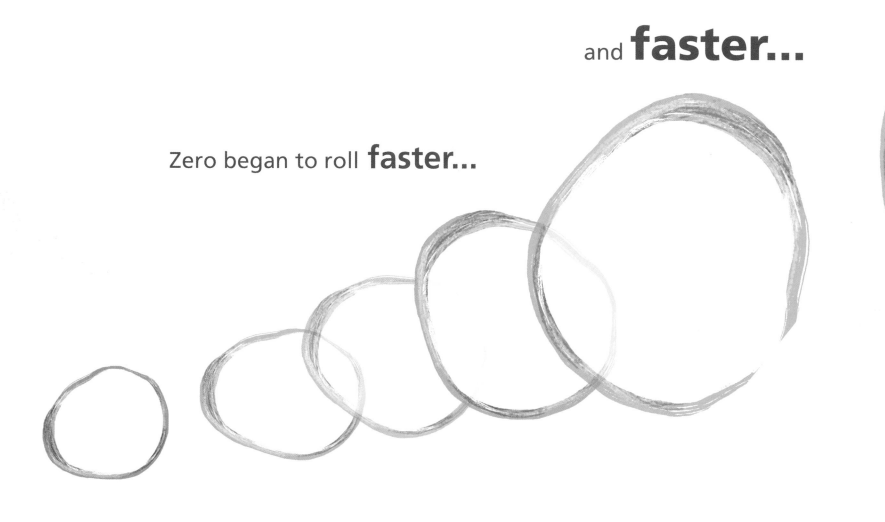

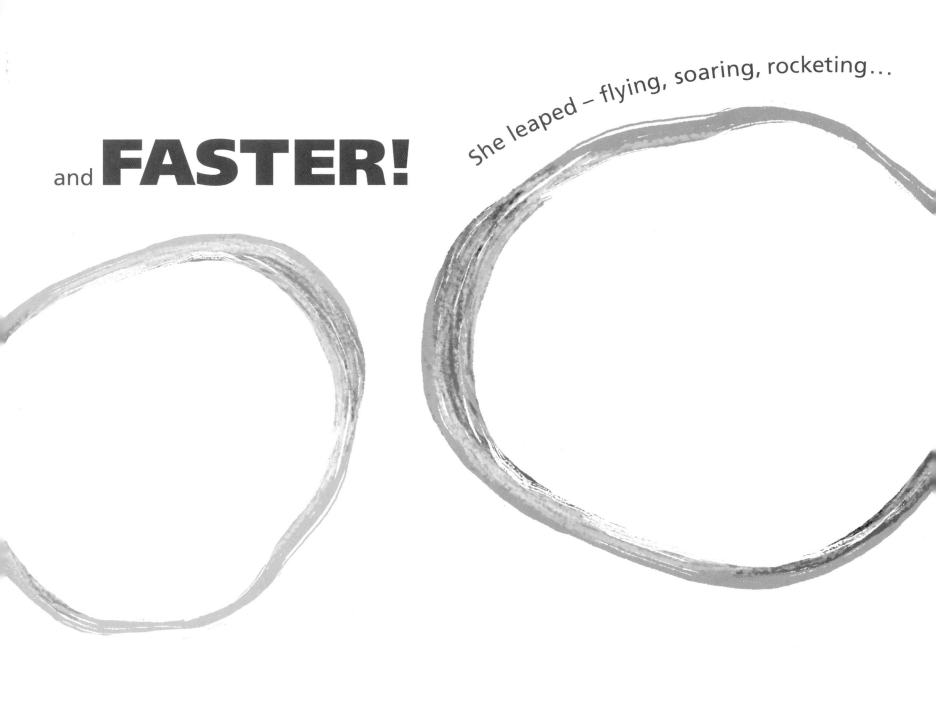

and **FASTER!**

She leaped – flying, soaring, rocketing…

right into **One**,

who knocked over **Two**,

who fell into **Three** and **Four**,

toppling **Five** and **Six**,

who crashed into **Seven** and **Eight**,

where they all ended up in a big pile on **Nine**.

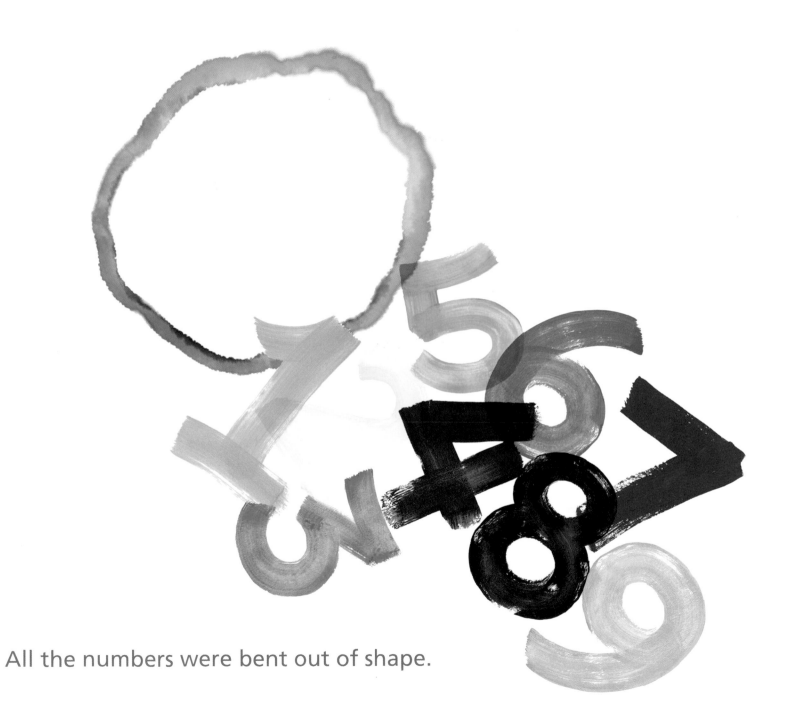

All the numbers were bent out of shape.

"It's no use trying," sobbed **Zero**. "I'll never have value. I'll never be part of the count," she said.

"It's what's *inside* that counts most," pointed out **Seven**.

Zero looked at herself.

"But…what if I don't have anything inside?"

"Every number has value," said **Seven**.

"Be *open*. You'll find a way."

Suddenly **Zero** saw herself in a new light.

"I'm not empty inside. I'm *open!*"

Zero rolled up to the numbers.

"I've thought of a way for us to count even *more!*" she said.

"Count more?" asked **Four**.

"Count us in!" exclaimed **Seven**.

"Lead the way!" said **One**.

"Everyone **counts!**" the numbers shouted.

Then she leaped up high and said, "Here's something new we can try!

Zero jumped in.

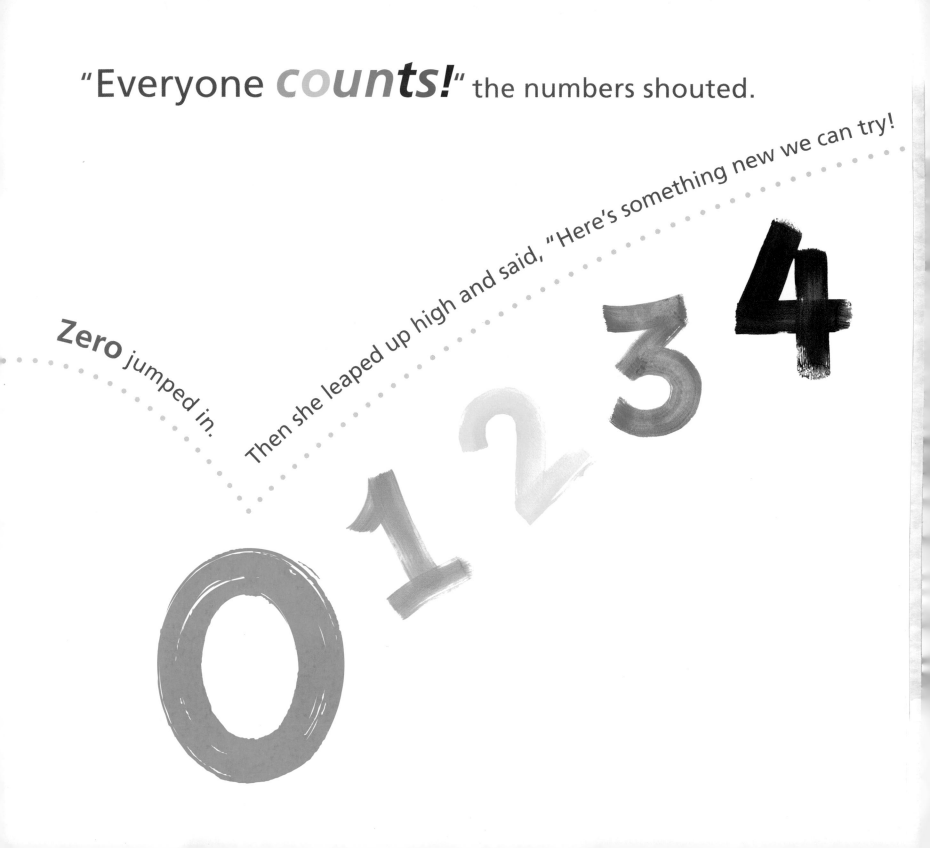

0 1 2 3 4

If we help each other **soar**, we can count even **more**! Let's **count again** starting with…"

5 6 7 8 9

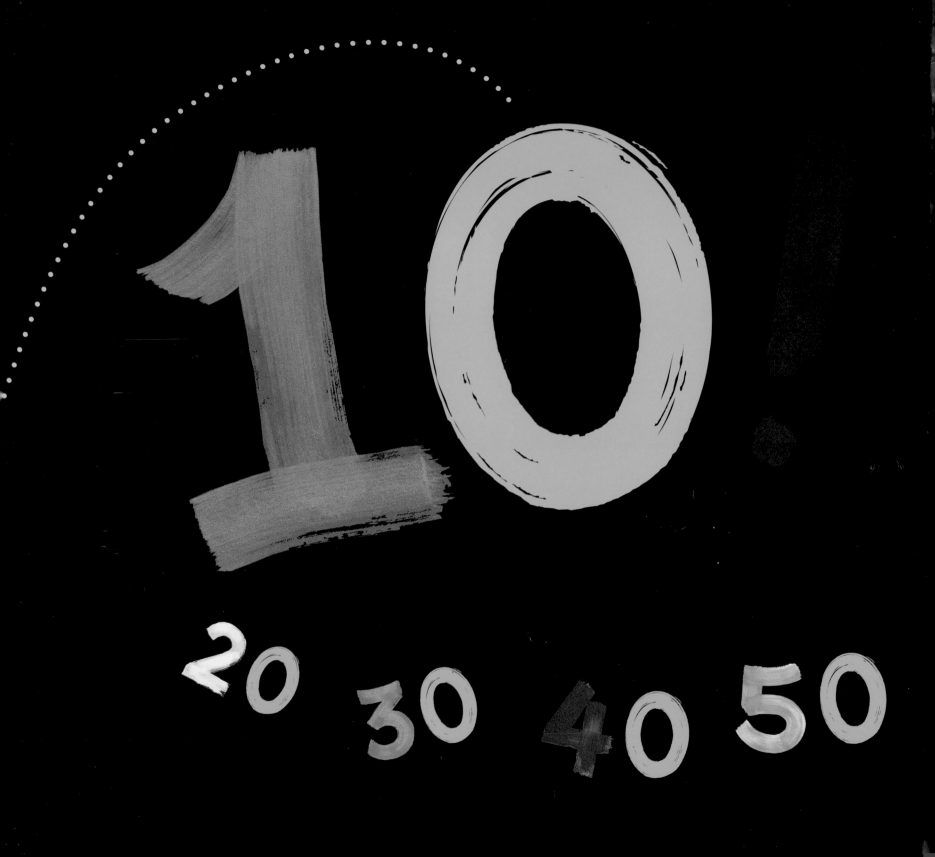

90...

80

70

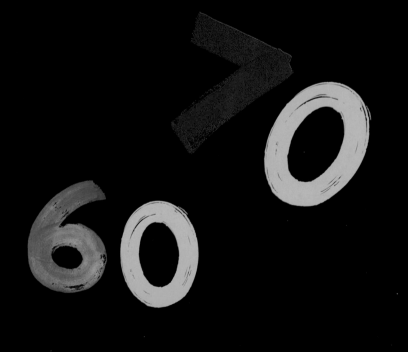

60

And what's next?

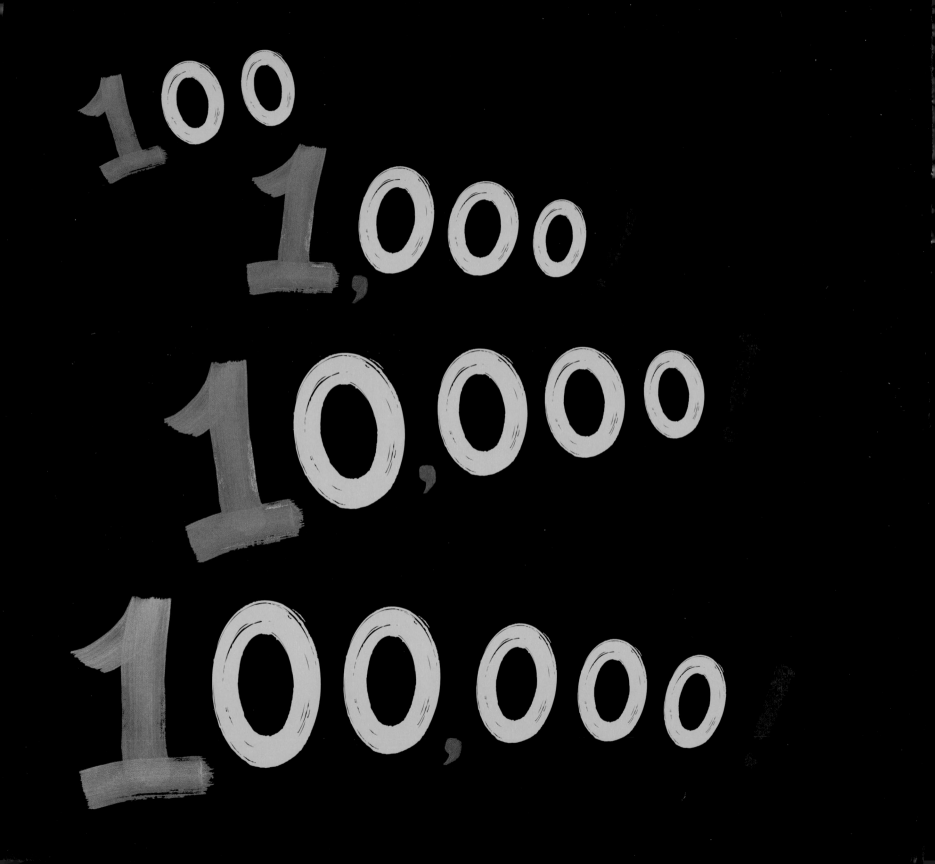

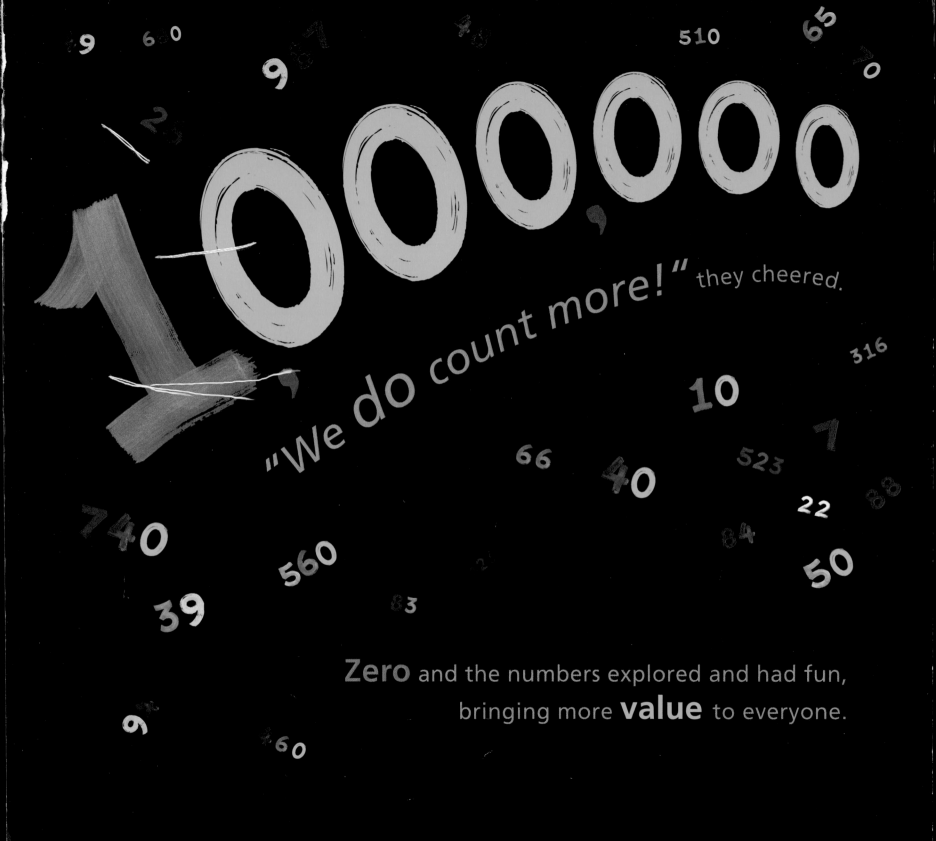

1,000,000

"We do count more!" they cheered.

Zero and the numbers explored and had fun,
bringing more **value** to everyone.

And this time when she looked at herself, she felt whole.

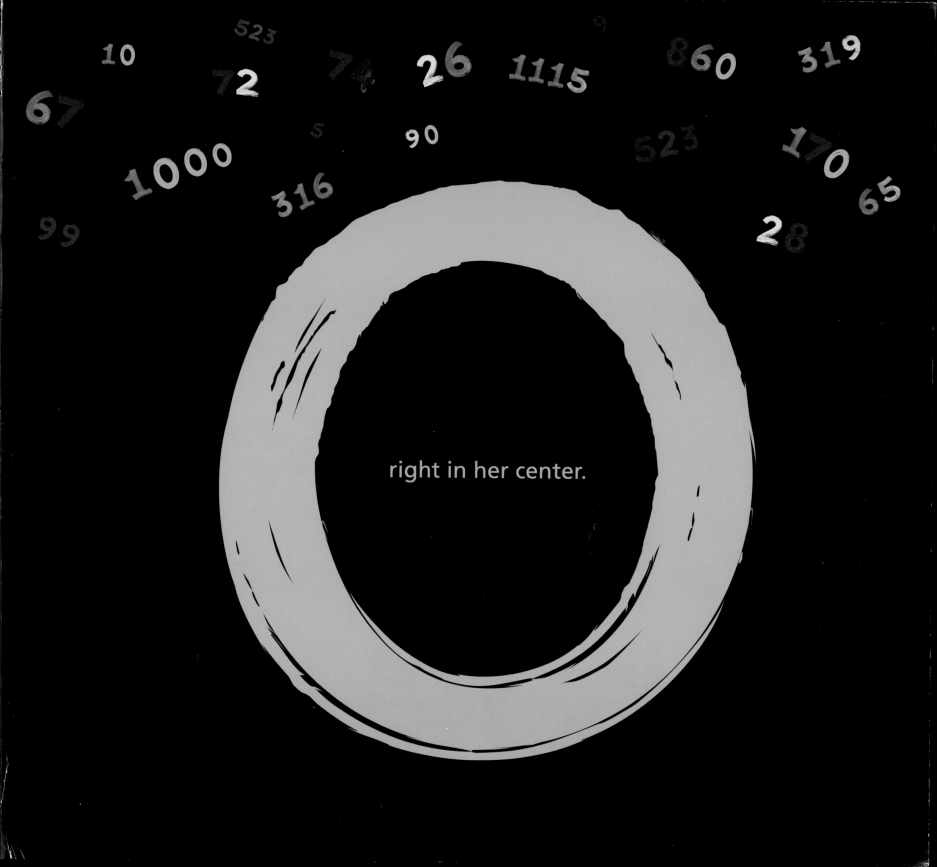

right in her center.

Thanks to
those of you who have
shared your powerful stories
of One with me, even
though we have never met.

You make me whole.

- K.O.